THE PILL

The Pill

A Thought-Provoking Collectible Short Story

Walter the Educator

Silent King Books

SILENT KING BOOKS

SKB

Registered Copyright ©2024. Walter the Educator.

All rights reserved. No part of this book may be reproduced in any manner whatsoever without written permission except in the case of brief quotations embodied in critical articles and reviews.

First Printing, 2024

Disclaimer
This book is a literary work; the story is not about specific persons, locations, situations, and/or circumstances unless mentioned in a historical context. Any resemblance to real persons, locations, situations, and/or circumstances is coincidental. This book is for entertainment and informational purposes only. The author and publisher offer this information without warranties expressed or implied. No matter the grounds, neither the author nor the publisher will be accountable for any losses, injuries, or other damages caused by the reader's use of this book. The use of this book acknowledges an understanding and acceptance of this disclaimer.

Imagine a world with no more sickness, where one pill could save anyone's life from sickness

THE PILL

In the heart of Waysium, a city renowned for its shimmering skyline and harmonious society, the invention of the Panacea Pill had revolutionized human existence. This small, iridescent capsule, the brainchild of the eminent scientist Dr. Elias Veritas, had eradicated all forms of illness. From common colds to terminal cancers, one pill could cure it all. Sickness, once a fundamental aspect of human experience, was now a relic of the past. The dawn of this new era saw a world brimming with vitality and an ever-increasing lifespan. People aged gracefully, unburdened by the debilitating ailments that had once plagued humanity. Hospitals transformed into research centers and wellness hubs, their sterile corridors echoing with laughter instead of anguish. Physicians became wellness consultants, guiding people toward optimal health rather than battling the onslaught of disease.

The Pill

Among the many inhabitants of Waysium, there was a young woman named Clara. A brilliant biochemist herself, she had dedicated her life to understanding the deeper implications of the Panacea Pill. Clara's parents had been among the last generation to know the fear of fatal illnesses, and she often heard stories of their struggles. These narratives fascinated her, sparking a curiosity that burned brightly despite the seemingly perfect world she inhabited. Clara's days were spent in a state-of-the-art laboratory, nestled in the heart of Waysium's research district. Her work focused on the long-term effects of the Panacea Pill, a subject that many deemed redundant given its miraculous success. Yet, Clara was driven by an insatiable need to comprehend the full spectrum of its impact on human biology and society.

The Pill

One evening, as the sun dipped below the horizon, casting a golden glow over the city, Clara made a startling discovery. While analyzing the cellular structure of patients who had consumed the pill, she noticed an anomaly. The cells, though healthy and vibrant, exhibited signs of an unusual mutation. It was subtle, almost imperceptible, but it was there—a faint trace of something that defied the known laws of biology. Intrigued and somewhat apprehensive, Clara delved deeper into her research. She meticulously reviewed countless data sets, comparing notes and running simulations. The anomaly persisted, a silent specter lurking beneath the surface of perfect health. Driven by a sense of duty and a thirst for knowledge, Clara decided to approach Dr. Veritas.

The Pill

Dr. Veritas, now in his twilight years, resided in a secluded estate on the outskirts of Waysium. Despite his age, his mind remained sharp, his eyes reflecting the brilliance that had once conceived the Panacea Pill. He welcomed Clara with a warm smile, his curiosity piqued by her unexpected visit. "Dr. Veritas," Clara began, her voice tinged with urgency, "I've discovered something unusual in the cellular structure of those who have taken the Panacea Pill. There's a mutation, subtle but consistent. I believe it warrants further investigation."

The Pill

Dr. Veritas listened intently, his expression thoughtful. After a moment, he spoke, his voice calm yet firm. "Clara, the Panacea Pill was designed to eliminate suffering. Its efficacy is undeniable. However, I always suspected that there might be unforeseen consequences. You've confirmed my long-held suspicions."

The Pill

Together, they embarked on a journey to unravel the mystery. Days turned into weeks as they pored over data, conducted experiments, and explored every conceivable angle. The anomaly, they discovered, was not harmful per se. Instead, it appeared to be an adaptive response, a way for the human body to cope with the absence of disease. The cells had evolved, developing new mechanisms to maintain equilibrium in a world where sickness no longer existed.

The Pill

This revelation posed profound questions about the nature of human existence. If the body could adapt to such a drastic change, what did it mean for the future of humanity? Would these mutations lead to unforeseen consequences, or were they simply a testament to the resilience of life? As Clara and Dr. Veritas delved deeper, they stumbled upon another startling revelation. The mutation, though benign, seemed to influence cognitive functions. People who had taken the Panacea Pill exhibited enhanced mental acuity, faster learning, and improved memory retention. It was as if the pill, in eradicating physical ailments, had inadvertently unlocked the latent potential of the human mind.

The Pill

This discovery sent ripples through the scientific community. The implications were staggering. The Panacea Pill had not only cured disease but had also catalyzed a new phase of human evolution. The very fabric of society began to shift as people embraced this newfound intellectual prowess. Creativity flourished, innovation soared, and the boundaries of human achievement expanded exponentially.

The Pill

Yet, amid this surge of progress, Clara couldn't shake a lingering unease. The mutation, while beneficial, represented a profound alteration of the human condition. The line between enhancement and essence blurred, raising ethical and philosophical questions that defied easy answers.

The Pill

In the midst of these contemplations, Clara encountered Samuel, a philosopher and ethicist known for his provocative ideas. Samuel had long been a critic of the Panacea Pill, arguing that its use fundamentally altered the human experience. He believed that suffering, though painful, was an essential aspect of life, fostering resilience, empathy, and a deeper understanding of existence.

The Pill

Intrigued by his perspective, Clara sought Samuel's counsel. They met in a quiet café, its walls adorned with vibrant murals depicting the history of Waysium. Over steaming cups of coffee, they engaged in a spirited debate. "Clara," Samuel began, his voice measured and reflective, "the Panacea Pill has undoubtedly transformed our world. But in eliminating suffering, we risk losing a crucial part of what it means to be human. Pain and illness, though undesirable, shape our character and forge our connections with one another."

The Pill

Clara listened intently, her mind racing. Samuel's words resonated with her, echoing the unease she had felt since discovering the mutation. "But Samuel," she countered, "the pill has also unlocked incredible potential. We've achieved things once thought impossible. Isn't that a testament to our adaptability and ingenuity?"

The Pill

Samuel nodded, acknowledging her point. "True, but at what cost? If we alter our fundamental nature, are we still truly human? Or are we becoming something else entirely?" This question lingered in Clara's mind as she continued her research. The Panacea Pill had undoubtedly ushered in a new era, but it also posed existential questions that defied simple answers. Clara realized that the path forward required a delicate balance, a synthesis of progress and preservation.

The Pill

Determined to address these complexities, Clara and Dr. Veritas proposed the establishment of an interdisciplinary council. Comprising scientists, ethicists, philosophers, and cultural leaders, this council would navigate the moral and societal implications of the Panacea Pill. Its mission would be to ensure that the benefits of the pill were harnessed responsibly while preserving the essence of humanity. The council's formation marked the beginning of a new chapter in Waysium's history. Dialogues flourished, bringing diverse perspectives to the forefront. The debates were passionate and often contentious, but they were driven by a shared commitment to the greater good.

The Pill

One of the council's first initiatives was the introduction of a voluntary program that encouraged individuals to experience life without the Panacea Pill for a designated period. This "Intermission Program" aimed to reintroduce elements of human vulnerability, fostering empathy and resilience. Participants shared their experiences, creating a tapestry of narratives that enriched the collective understanding of what it meant to be human.

The Pill

As the years passed, Waysium evolved into a society that embraced both the advantages of the Panacea Pill and the invaluable lessons of human vulnerability. The city thrived, its inhabitants achieving unprecedented heights of intellectual and creative prowess while remaining deeply connected to the core aspects of their humanity.

Clara, now a respected leader in both the scientific and philosophical communities, reflected on the journey that had brought her to this point. The Panacea Pill had been a catalyst for change, challenging humanity to redefine itself in the face of boundless potential. It had sparked a renaissance of thought, bridging the gap between progress and preservation.

The Pill

In the twilight of her life, Clara stood on the balcony of her apartment, overlooking the vibrant city of Waysium. The skyline shimmered with the promise of a future where humanity's essence and intellect coexisted in harmonious equilibrium. The Panacea Pill had indeed eradicated sickness, but it had also prompted a profound exploration of what it meant to live a truly fulfilling life.

The Pill

As Clara gazed at the twinkling stars, a soft knock echoed through her apartment. She turned to find Lucas, a young prodigy she had mentored since his days as an intern in her laboratory. His eyes sparkled with excitement and a hint of concern.

The Pill

"Clara, I've made a breakthrough," Lucas said, holding a tablet loaded with complex data charts and graphs. "It's about the mutation. I think I've found a way to understand its full potential and implications." Intrigued, Clara invited Lucas inside, and they sat together, poring over the information. Lucas explained that he had discovered a secondary layer of the mutation, one that not only enhanced cognitive abilities but also influenced emotional responses. This aspect, which had previously eluded detection, appeared to heighten empathy, compassion, and social cohesion.

The Pill

"This could be revolutionary," Clara mused. "But it also raises new questions about our autonomy and the natural spectrum of human emotions." Lucas nodded. "Exactly. If we're enhancing these traits through the pill, are we still experiencing genuine emotions, or are they artificially amplified?" Clara and Lucas decided to present their findings to the council. The interdisciplinary council had become a cornerstone of Waysium's society, guiding ethical considerations and ensuring balanced progress. As they stood before the council members, Clara felt a sense of déjà vu, recalling the initial presentation of the mutation years ago.

The Pill

"Esteemed members," Clara began, "Lucas has uncovered a new dimension to the mutation caused by the Panacea Pill. It appears to enhance not only cognitive abilities but also emotional responses, particularly empathy and social cohesion."

The Pill

The council members listened intently, their faces reflecting a mix of curiosity and concern. After Clara and Lucas finished their presentation, a lively debate ensued. Dr. Emilia Hart, a prominent ethicist, voiced a critical perspective. "While enhanced empathy and social cohesion are desirable, we must consider the implications for personal autonomy. Are we subtly altering our free will and the authenticity of our emotions?"

The Pill

Samuel, the philosopher, added his thoughts. "This discovery challenges our understanding of human nature. It's crucial that we tread carefully. Enhanced traits might lead to a more harmonious society, but we must preserve the essence of genuine human experience." The council decided to commission a comprehensive study to explore the long-term effects of these emotional enhancements. Clara and Lucas would lead the research, collaborating with experts from various fields to ensure a holistic approach.

The Pill

As the study progressed, Clara found herself reflecting on her own emotions and relationships. She had always prided herself on her analytical mind, but now she wondered how much of her empathy and compassion had been influenced by the Panacea Pill. These introspective moments deepened her resolve to uncover the truth, not just for the sake of science, but for the integrity of human experience.

The Pill

Months passed, and the study yielded fascinating insights. The enhanced empathy and social cohesion were indeed present, but their effects varied among individuals. Some people embraced these changes, finding greater fulfillment and connection in their lives. Others felt a sense of dissonance, struggling to reconcile their enhanced emotions with their sense of self.

The Pill

One evening, while reviewing the latest data, Clara received a call from an old friend, Evelyn. Evelyn had been a renowned artist before the Panacea Pill's advent, her work celebrated for its raw emotional depth. They hadn't spoken in years, and Clara was surprised by the sudden contact.

The Pill

"Clara, I need to talk to you," Evelyn said, her voice tinged with urgency. "There's something I've been struggling with, something I think you'll understand." They met at Evelyn's studio, a place filled with vibrant canvases and sculptures. Evelyn's art had always been a reflection of her soul, and Clara could see the conflict etched into her latest pieces.

The Pill

"Clara," Evelyn began, "ever since I started taking the Panacea Pill, I've felt different. My creativity has flourished, but I can't shake the feeling that my emotions are not entirely my own. It's as if the pill has reshaped my very essence, and I'm losing touch with the authentic source of my inspiration." Clara listened, her heart heavy with understanding. Evelyn's struggle mirrored the broader questions she had been grappling with in her research. "Evelyn, your experience is valuable. It highlights the need to understand the full spectrum of the pill's impact on our emotional and creative selves."

The Pill

Together, they devised a plan to explore the artistic and emotional dimensions of the mutation. Evelyn would undergo a temporary cessation of the Panacea Pill, documenting her creative process and emotional journey during this period. This experiment aimed to provide insights into the nuances of human experience in a world transformed by the pill.

The Pill

Evelyn's journey was both enlightening and challenging. As she weaned off the pill, she experienced a resurgence of raw, unfiltered emotions. Her art took on a new intensity, capturing the essence of her internal struggle. She felt a renewed connection to her authentic self, but also faced the physical vulnerabilities that the pill had shielded her from.

The Pill

Clara and the council monitored Evelyn's progress closely, their findings contributing to the broader understanding of the pill's impact. The results were profound: while the Panacea Pill enhanced certain traits, it also introduced a subtle but significant shift in the authenticity of human experience. The study revealed that a balanced approach, integrating the benefits of the pill with periods of natural vulnerability, could offer a more holistic and authentic way of living.

The Pill

Waysium began to embrace this new paradigm. The Intermission Program was expanded, allowing citizens to experience intervals without the pill, fostering resilience and genuine emotional depth. This approach led to a richer, more nuanced society, where the interplay between enhancement and authenticity became a cornerstone of the human experience.

The Pill

Clara's work earned her international acclaim, and she continued to mentor young scientists like Lucas, nurturing a new generation committed to ethical and balanced progress. The interdisciplinary council evolved into a global institution, guiding societies worldwide as they navigated the complexities of technological and biological advancements.

The Pill

As the years rolled by, Clara witnessed the fruits of their efforts. Waysium thrived, a beacon of innovation, empathy, and authenticity. People lived longer, healthier lives, but they also valued the depth of genuine human experience. The Panacea Pill, once seen as a miracle cure, had become a tool for enhancing life's potential while preserving its essence.

The Pill

In her twilight years, Clara found herself once again on her balcony, reflecting on the journey that had shaped her life and the world around her. She felt a deep sense of fulfillment, knowing that they had navigated the delicate balance between progress and preservation. One evening, as the city below buzzed with life and laughter, Clara was joined by Lucas, now a distinguished scientist and philosopher in his own right. They sat together, watching the stars and contemplating the future.

The Pill

"Clara," Lucas said, breaking the comfortable silence, "do you ever wonder what's next? What other mysteries lie beyond our current understanding?" Clara smiled, her eyes twinkling with the same curiosity that had driven her throughout her life. "Always, Lucas. The quest for knowledge and understanding is endless. But I'm confident that, with the foundations we've built, future generations will navigate those mysteries with wisdom and integrity."

The Pill

As they gazed at the stars, Clara felt a profound sense of peace. The world had changed, but it had also found a way to honor its past, embracing both innovation and the timeless essence of human experience. In a world where sickness no longer existed, humanity had discovered new ways to grow, connect, and thrive, ever curious and ever resilient.

The Pill

As the stars twinkled above, Clara felt a deep sense of gratitude. The journey had been fraught with challenges, but it had led to a deeper understanding of the human condition. In a world where sickness no longer existed, humanity had discovered new ways to grow, connect, and thrive. The story of Waysium was one of resilience, adaptability, and the unending quest for a balanced and meaningful existence.

The Pill

ABOUT THE CREATOR

Walter the Educator is one of the pseudonyms for Walter Anderson. Formally educated in Chemistry, Business, and Education, he is an educator, an author, a diverse entrepreneur, and he is the son of a disabled war veteran. "Walter the Educator" shares his time between educating and creating. He holds interests and owns several creative projects that entertain, enlighten, enhance, and educate, hoping to inspire and motivate you.

Follow, find new works, and stay up to date
with Walter the Educator™
at WaltertheEducator.com

www.ingramcontent.com/pod-product-compliance
Lightning Source LLC
LaVergne TN
LVHW051922060526
838201LV00060B/4127